Little Red Riding Hood

Retold by Susanna Davidson

Illustrated by Mike Gordon

Reading Consultant: Alison Kelly
Roehampton University

Once upon a time there was a kind little girl called Little Red Riding Hood.

She always wore a bright red cloak with a bright red hood.

I love it so much I never take it off.

Little Red Riding Hood lived with her mother on the edge of some deep, dark woods.

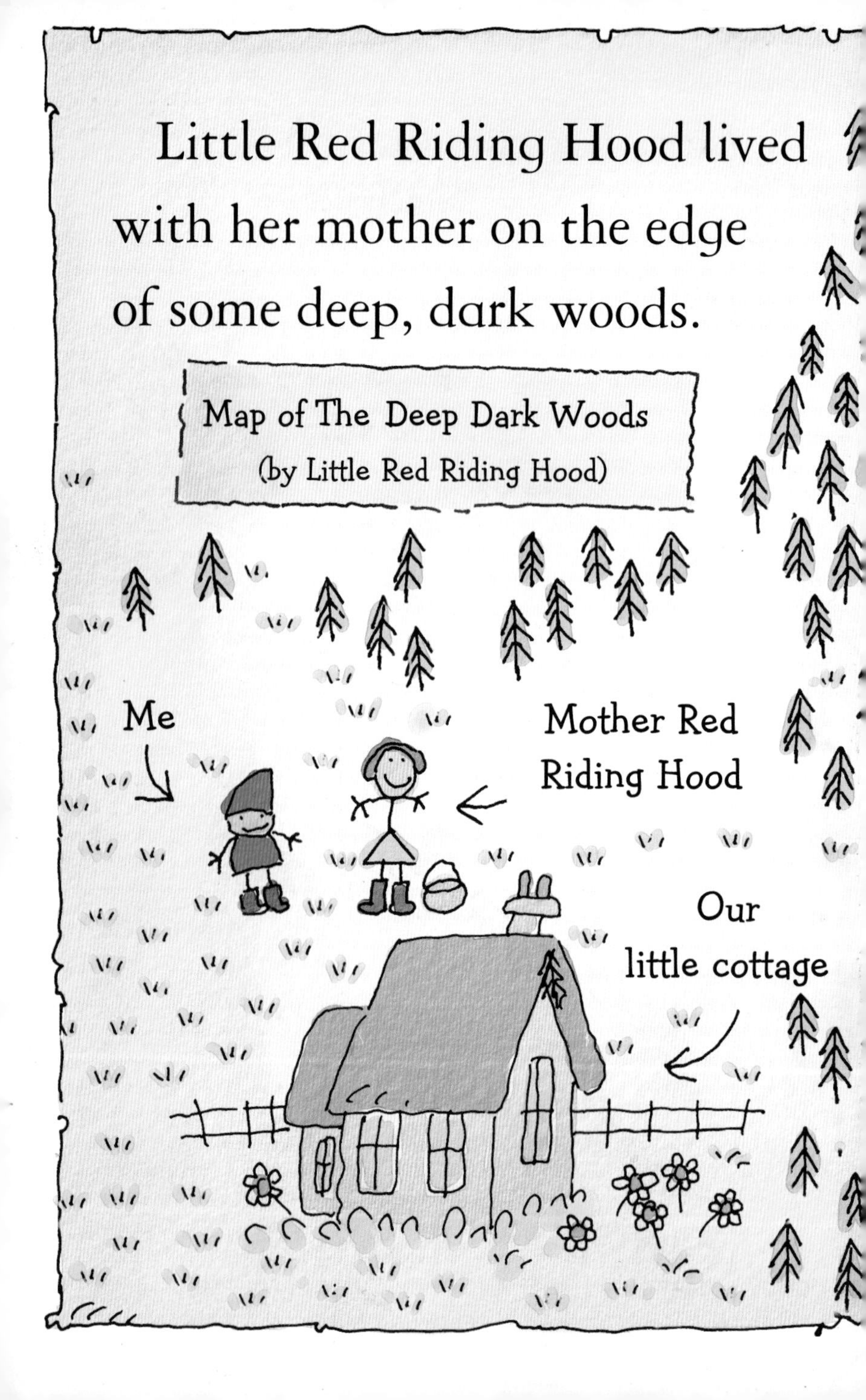

One day, Little Red Riding Hood's mother gave her a pot of vegetable soup.

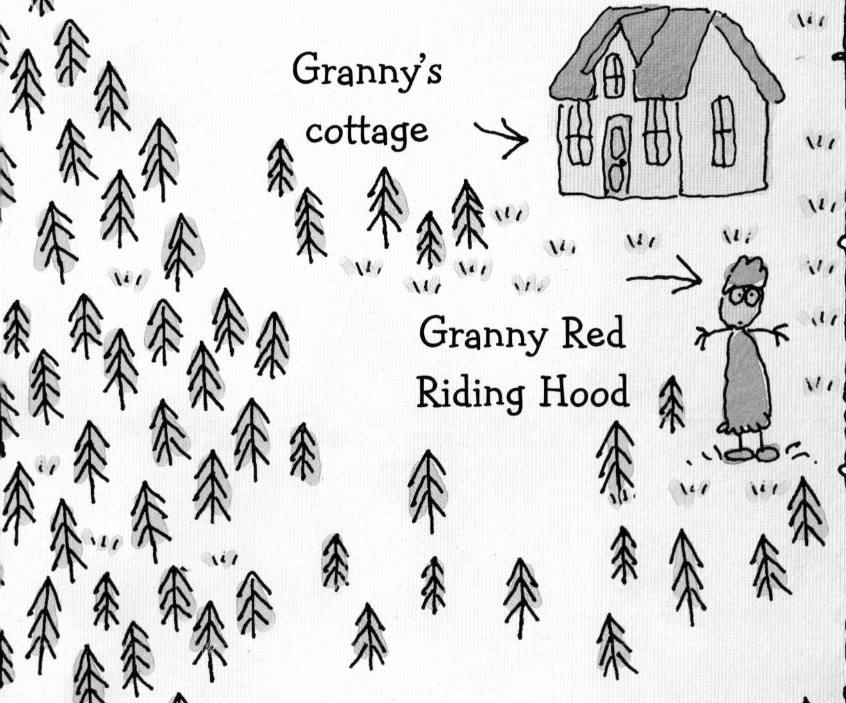

Granny's cottage

Granny Red Riding Hood

"Take this to your grandmother," she said. "She's not feeling well."

"But remember the Rules of the Woods," her mother added.

"I will," promised Little Red Riding Hood and she set off.

At first, the sun shone and the birds sang.

Little Red Riding Hood hummed a little tune...

bent down to tie her shoelace...

skipped along the path...

and stopped to smell the flowers.

"Good morning, Little Red Riding Hood," called a woodcutter.

"Good morning," said Little Red Riding Hood, waving to him.

Little Red Riding Hood walked deeper and deeper into the woods...

It grew darker and darker.

Then the sun hid behind the clouds and it got darker still.

So Little Red Riding Hood didn't see the wolf waiting for her on the path.

And the wolf didn't see Little Red Riding Hood either.

Little Red Riding Hood stepped on the wolf's tail...

then on his paw...

and dropped her basket **SMACK!** on his head.

“Look where you’re going!” said the wolf, huffily.

“But you were in the middle of the path,” said Little Red Riding Hood.

She had forgotten the rule –

Don't talk to wolves.

"What have you got in that basket?" asked the wolf, hungrily.

"Vegetable soup," replied Little Red Riding Hood. "I'm taking it to my grandmother."

"Vegetables?" cried the wolf. "How revolting!"

"Wolves only eat juicy, red meat. I never touch *vegetables*," he added.

The wolf was about to gobble up Little Red Riding Hood. But then he had an idea.

"Perhaps I can eat Little Red Riding Hood *and* her grandmother!" he thought.

He put on his softest voice. "Where does your grandmother live?" he asked.

"In the cottage on the other side of the woods," said Little Red Riding Hood.

"How perfect!" thought the wolf, rubbing his tummy. "How delicious!"

"Why don't you take her some flowers?" he suggested.

"What a kind wolf you are," said Little Red Riding Hood.

So Little Red Riding Hood
left the path to look
for flowers...

and the wolf raced off to the
grandmother's house.

He knocked lightly on the door. Tap! Tap! Tap!

"Who's there?" asked the grandmother.

"Your granddaughter, Little Red Riding Hood," squeaked the wolf.

"I've brought you some lovely vegetable soup."

“Let yourself in,” said the grandmother.

The wolf leaped into the room.

He gobbled up Little Red Riding Hood's grandmother.

Then he climbed into bed to wait for Little Red Riding Hood.

Soon he heard a knock at the door.

"Who's there?" he said.

"Your granddaughter, Little Red Riding Hood."

"Let yourself in," called the wolf.

He pulled on the grandmother's cap and hid under the blankets.

"I've brought you some vegetable soup," said Little Red Riding Hood.

"Lovely," snarled the wolf. "I mean *lovely*!" he added in a squeak.

"Put the basket on the stool and come and sit next to me."

Little Red Riding Hood looked at her grandmother. She looked again.

"Oh Grandmother," she said. "What big ears you have."

"All the better to hear you with," said the wolf.

Little Red Riding Hood came closer to the bed. "Oh Grandmother," she said. "What big eyes you have."

"All the better to see you with," said the wolf.

Little Red Riding Hood came closer still.

"Oh Grandmother," she said. "What big hairy hands you have."

"All the better to hug you with," said the wolf.

Little Red Riding Hood was now standing right next to the bed.

"But Grandmother," she cried, "what big sharp teeth you have."

"All the better to eat you with," snapped the wolf.

He jumped out of bed and gobbled up Little Red Riding Hood.

"Full at last!" he said, licking his lips. Then he lay down on the bed to sleep.

As the wolf slept, he snored... very loudly.

He snored so loudly the woodcutter heard him. "I've never heard the old woman snore *that* loudly," he thought.

“I’ll just make sure she’s okay.”

But the woodcutter couldn’t see the grandmother anywhere – only a very fat wolf.

"Oh no!" thought the woodcutter. "The wolf's eaten the old woman."

Just then, the woodcutter had an idea.

"Perhaps the old woman is still inside you. I might be able to save her."

He picked up some scissors. Then he snipped open the wolf's tummy.

Snip, snip... He saw a bright red hood. Snip, snip... Little Red Riding Hood's head popped out.

"Keep cutting!" she cried. "Grandmother's still in there."

Snippety-snip, faster and faster... The woodcutter kept cutting until Grandmother popped out too.

Quick as a flash, Little Red Riding Hood ran outside and picked up lots of stones.

The woodcutter put them in the wolf's tummy

and the grandmother sewed the tummy up.

Then the wolf woke up. He tried to sneak out of the door, but the stones rattled inside him.

"Now everyone can hear you coming," said the woodcutter, laughing.

"But I'll never catch anyone," cried the wolf.

"Exactly!" said the woodcutter.

"You'll just have to eat *vegetables* instead," said Little Red Riding Hood.

The wolf never ate another person.

As for Little Red Riding Hood, she never, ever talked to a wolf again.

Little Red Riding Hood was first written down by two brothers, Jacob and Wilhelm Grimm, about two hundred years ago. The Grimm brothers lived in Germany and liked collecting lots of very grim stories.

Series editor: Lesley Sims
Designed by Louise Flutter
Cover design: Russell Punter

First published in 2006 by Usborne Publishing Ltd., Usborne House, 83-85 Saffron Hill, London EC1N 8RT, England. www.usborne.com

Printed in China. UE. First published in America in 2006.